This book is dedicated to my mom and dad, and my sons, David and Michael.

With a special thank you to my wonderful and supportive husband, awesome volunteers and kind supporters.

Maria's Cupcakes for the Homeless

The proceeds of this book will enable us to continue with the mission of Maria's Birthday Wishes for the Homeless, a 501(c)(3), non-profit organization that remembers and celebrates the birthdays of those who call the streets their home. By celebrating birthdays of the homeless, we are able to bring acknowledgment, smiles, hope and self worth to the less fortunate.

"Working together to change lives one cupcake at a time."

Please visit www.mariasbirthdaywishesforthehomeless.org to learn more about the organization and how you can help.

Tutti's Adventures in Cupcake Land

To Austen & Nora;

Be Kind today so you can shine all day!

Maria Wossek

Once upon a time in a far off land
where no one seemed to care,
was a pink-and-white bakery shop
that had a special flair.

It had a flair for baking cupcakes
full of love and bringing joy
to anyone who tasted them –
man or woman, girl or boy.

Sitting prettily inside the shop,
protected by a glass case,
was an array of delicious and delightful
and uniquely flavored cupcakes.

Chocolate and strawberry,
cinnamon and vanilla cream,
all tucked in cozily beside each other,
making the most beautiful team.

They were all unique
and pretty as gems,
and brought wide shiny smiles
to those who ate them.

Tutti was the leader of the team,
dressed to impress with a white velvet cream.
Next to Tutti was Cutie,
a luscious strawberry queen.

Then came Smarty,
a non-fat chocolate cupcake
made with special ingredients
and carefully baked.

Beside her sat Nutty,
a peanut-buttery treat.
He was the comical cupcake
that all loved to eat.

Mysterly was made with
a top-secret recipe.
Her flavor changed each day
to keep it a mystery.

Finally came Smiley,
made from cinammon and spice.
He gave zest to the rest,
always comforting and nice.

But in a dark alley corner
on a lonely nearby street,
waited Greedy the garbage can,
who loved cupcakes he could eat.

He loved to eat anything
people would throw to waste.
With trash or treats
he'd quickly stuff his face.

He ate all through the day
and all through the night,
filling up his trash can
much to his delight.

One thing especially that Greedy
could not resist,
was the taste of happy cupcakes
on his garbage-can lips.

He stayed up all hours
on his dark, lonely street,
waiting for cupcakes
he could make his own treat.

Because if no one came
into the bakery each day,
that night old Greedy
would chomp the cupcakes away.

It was almost night,
the sky was navy blue.
Tutti, Cutie, Smiley, Nutty,
Mysterly, and Smarty all knew,

That if no one came
to pick them up before the night would fall,
selfish old Greedy
would come and eat them all.

Wait, what was this light?
It was shining so bright!
It entered the bakery
along with the night!

The glass case was opened
and things got sort of scary.
But there was no need to fear –

for it was the Cupcake Fairy!

With her colorful pink apron
and soft fairy wings of white,
The Cupcake Fairy stood before them
ready to transport them into the night.

With a sparkling smile
and a diamond cupcake crown,
she swooped into the shop
and took the cupcakes into town

She delivered those cupcakes
to people much in need;
leaving Greedy the Garbage Can
with only scraps upon which to feed.

The kind-hearted Cupcake Fairy
got straight down to work.
She couldn't waste a moment
in passing out the perks.

Tutti, the leader,
was the first of the cupcake team,
who was given to Tom,
the homeless man with a dream.

Cutie gave smiles
in true strawberry style,
to honor the birthday
of Tom's only child.

Smiley the cupcake
made everyone laugh
with his cinnamon cheer –
well, they all had a blast!

Nutty the cupcake
was long on delight –
his kindness and goofiness
made everyone bright.

Though Mysterly thought
she'd not help out a lot,
she was the extra cupcake
for the one birthday forgot.

And Smarty concluded
that their purpose was
to do unto others
what we'd want done to us.

The bakery's most secret
and special recipe
was a pinch of hope
for people in need.

With a cup of caring and kindness
and a half-cup of laughter
both the cupcakes and people
learned to live happily ever after.

And in our hearts
a seed of kindness was planted
And our souls were filled
with care, love and richness,
And our hands became like trees
with plenty fruitful gifts for all people,
And for that we experience giving
And that is truly living.

– Maria Wassef

Maria Wassef – Writer

Maria Wassef grew up in a home with an amazing mother, father and sister, where there was a focus on love and equality. She attended school at Villa Maria Academy with Immaculate Heart of Mary Catholic nuns where she learned discipline, faith, and the reinforcement of the concept of living a life based around giving.

After Maria left home she understood the depths of her mother's love and caring when she had her own two beautiful sons. Through her experiences, she learned that life brings you infinite possibilities to do good. Maria experienced numerous instances where life wasn't always fair, and in those moments truly understood the meaning and value of having a kind and giving heart.

Real accomplishments come from a combination of hard work and miracles. The love you carry in your heart can manifest itself into invaluable experiences for others in need, and only grows stronger with belief and faith.

This notion has become her fundamental core of existence; knowing how much of a blessing and honor it is to serve another human being in need.

Berenice Pignano

The llustrator was born in Lima, Peru in 1977. She received her BFA from the Florida State University College of Fine Arts in 2001.

Pignano has exhibited in the U.S. including shows at the Florida State Museum of Fine Arts, Gadsden Art Center, OM, and Raymond James, in Tallahassee. Her work has been featured in the Tallahassee Democrat Lime Light. Berenice Pignano lives and works in Tallahassee, Florida.

Michael Wassef – Musician

Born in Miami, FL, in 1986, Michael is a professional musician who self-taught himself piano by ear at the age of three. Ever since then, music has been an integral part of his life.

At the age of 13, he formed and fronted the rock band, Later Days, and has played at prominent venues like Universal CityWalk in Hollywood, CA as well as the Staples Center. As a songwriter, Michael has enjoyed success, licensing several of his songs to major cable networks such as: MTV, E! Entertainment, Vh1, Fox, Oxygen Network, and A&E. He is also a member of the Screen Actors Guild and grantmanship certified.

Please download your free mp3,

"Dreams to Life – The Tutti Version"

at the following link:

http://bit.ly/Njr8YG
(case sensitive)

or using the QR code above.

It doesn't matter who you are; be kind today and you will shine like a star all day
It is important for a child to learn kindness at a young age. And kindness will be present in
your heart whenever you sing along to this song.
"Dreams to Life – The Tutti Version" was produced and written by Mike Wassef.

Please go to:

www.cupcakekindness.com

and get into the "Cupcake Fairy's Kindness List"

All you have to do – is do something nice for someone!

Prizes and Gifts are awarded monthly to the kindest gestures the Cupcake Fairy sees!

For more information contact Maria@cupcakekindness.com

18009403R00025

Made in the USA
San Bernardino, CA
23 December 2014